D0531206

Tips for Reading Together

Children learn best when reading is fun.

- Talk about the title and the pictures on the cover.
- Look through the pictures together so your child can see what the story is about.
- Read the story to your child, placing your finger under the words as you read.
- Have fun finding the hidden starfish.
- Read the story again and encourage your child to join in.
- Give lots of praise as your child reads with you.

Children enjoy reading stories again and again. This helps to build their confidence.

Have fun!

Find the starfish hidden in every picture.

Funny Fish

Written by Cynthia Rider
Illustrated by Alex Brychta

OXFORD
UNIVERSITY PRESS

Mum Dad Biff

Chip Kipper Floppy

Kipper was fishing.

He got a hat.

Biff was fishing.

She got a crab.

Chip was fishing.

He got an octopus!

Mum was fishing.

She got a bucket.

Dad was fishing.

He got a boot.

SPLASH!

Floppy got a fish!

Think about the story

Tangled lines

Follow the lines to see who gets the fish.

Useful common words repeated in this story and other books at Level 1.

a got he she was

Names in this story: Mum Dad Biff Chip Kipper Floppy

More books for you to enjoy

Level 1: Getting Ready

Level 2: Starting to Read

Level 3: Becoming a Reader

Level 4: Building Confidence

Level 5: Reading with Confidence

OXFORD
UNIVERSITY PRESS
Great Clarendon Street,
Oxford OX2 6DP

Text © Cynthia Rider 2005
Illustrations © Alex Brychta 2005
Designed by Andy Wilson

First published 2005
All rights reserved

British Library Cataloguing
in Publication Data available

ISBN 978-0-19-838554-7

10 9 8 7 6 5 4

Printed in China by Imago

Have more fun with Read at Home

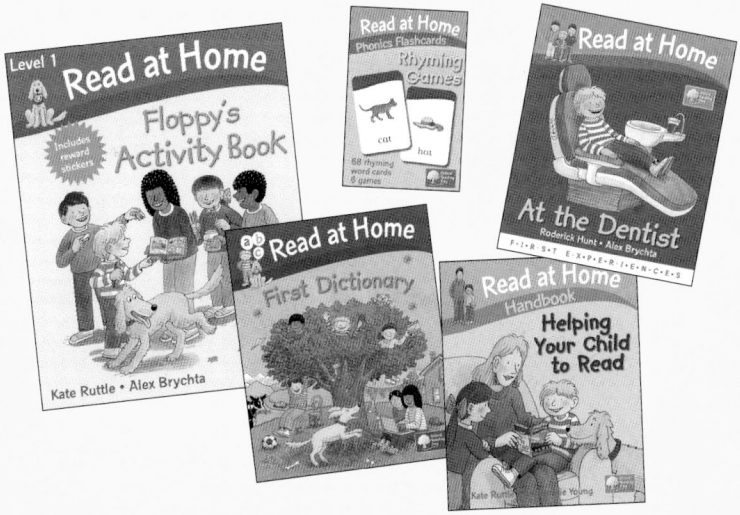